Now 15 years old, Ben is once again forced to turn to the Omnitrix to help fight a new and more sinister threat – the HighBreed, DNAliens and the Forever Knights, who team up to take over the world.

The watch-like Omnitrix has re-programmed itself and has a complete set of ten, brand new alien choices for Ben to get to grips with. Helped by his cousin Gwen with her magical powers and Ben's former enemy, Kevin E. Levin, Ben is soon all set to go hero once again!

NOW READ ON . . .

MEET THE CHARACTERS

Ben Tennyson
Always ready to go hero

Gwen Tennyson
Ben's cousin, with her
own superpowers

Kevin E. Levin
A good guy now, with
absorbing powers

Grandpa Max
Tough and brave,
but out on his own

Humungousaur
Ben's largest alien, you
wouldn't cross him

ChromaStone
One super-tough,
crystal guy

Jet Ray
Can fly and swim, and
fire shock blasts

Big Chill
This cool guy can
freeze anything

Mike Morningstar
This glittery guy isn't all
that he seems

HighBreed
The most serious threat
that Ben has ever seen

DNAliens
Creepy guys, servants
of the HighBreed

EGMONT

We bring stories to life

First published in Great Britain 2009
by Egmont UK Limited
239 Kensington High Street,
London W8 6SA

Adapted by Barry Hutchison

ISBN 978 1 4052 5006 1

1 3 5 7 9 10 8 6 4 2

Printed and bound in Great Britain

The Forest Stewardship Council (FSC) is an international,
non-governmental organisation dedicated to promoting
responsible management of the world's forests. FSC operates
a system of forest certification and product labelling that
allows consumers to identify wood and wood-based products
from well managed forests.

For more information about Egmont's paper buying policy,
please visit www.egmont.co.uk/ethicalpublishing
For more information about the FSC, please visit their
website at www.fsc.org

ALL THAT GLITTERS
+
MAX OUT

ALL THAT GLITTERS

CHAPTER ONE

A MESSAGE FROM MAX

Lucy stood there in the near-darkness, her neat school uniform doing little to protect her from the cold evening air. Right before her was the thick, heavy door of a sprawling mansion.

'Let me in,' she pleaded, as her fists pounded against the varnished timber of the door. She could feel her hand beginning to bruise. 'I need to see you,' she begged, her arms sagging as her strength began to fade. 'Please.'

Lucy rested her head against the door. She was tired. So very tired. If she could just rest a moment then maybe she'd figure out some way to . . .

With a faint click the porch light flicked on, illuminating the girl on the step. An excited gasp slipped from her lips as she stepped back and raised her head. A lock was turned; a bolt was slid back. Lucy watched the door as it inched slowly open with a **CREEEEEAK**.

There was no light inside the house. As Lucy moved to step through the door something flashed in the dark. A round mouth ringed with rows of razor sharp teeth lunged suddenly from the shadows, cutting off Lucy's scream before it even had a chance to start.

A short time later, not too far away, three teenagers discussed their plans for the evening. There was a school test coming up, and all three of them were worried.

'I'll meet you guys at the library after dinner,' suggested one boy. 'About – '

A sound from somewhere along the street stopped him in his tracks. All three teenagers listened. There it was again: a low moan that sent a shiver along their spines.

The sound of a shuffled footstep scuffing on the pavement made them jump. They came face to face with a young girl in school uniform.

Only the girl didn't look young at all. Her skin was grey, stretched tightly over her sunken cheekbones. Her body was frail and withered, and her dark eyes had not a trace of life in them.

The three friends turned and ran, screaming in terror, as the zombie that had been Lucy slowly shuffled off into the night.

Grandpa Max's face was blurred and a little distorted, but his voice was crystal clear. Ben sat on the kerb outside a corner shop, studying the tiny hologram of his grandfather. When the message ended he hit the button to play the recording again.

'If you've found this, you're in pretty deep,' Grandpa Max's hologram warned. 'There's a lot I can't reveal yet, but here's one thing I can. You can't go it alone.'

'By now you're probably meeting some of the other Plumbers' kids. But you have to find more. You need to put together a team.'

A few parking spaces away from Ben, Kevin was leaning on the bonnet of his car. Gwen, Ben's cousin, stood beside Kevin. Her arms were folded and she had a serious expression on her face. Kevin knew what that look meant. There was trouble ahead.

'Think we should be worried about him?' Kevin asked, nodding across to Ben, who had started to replay the recording again. 'He's been watching that thing for hours.'

Gwen didn't reply, but Kevin noticed her foot had begun to tap impatiently on the pavement. That was never a good sign.

'Problem?' he asked, trying to remember anything he might have done to upset her.

'Why haven't you asked me out?' Gwen suddenly demanded.

'What?' Kevin spluttered.

'You heard me. We spend all of our time together and you obviously like me.'

'Ha!' laughed Kevin, quickly turning his head away.

'You do,' Gwen insisted. 'I see you watching me when you think I'm not looking.'

Kevin opened his mouth to argue, but Gwen wasn't going to give him the chance.

'And I like you,' she smiled. 'Most of the time. So I'm asking you again – '

'See, that's the problem,' snapped Kevin. 'You're asking me. A guy does the asking.'

'Yeah?' asked Gwen with a smirk. 'When?'

'Don't push me,' Kevin said.

Gwen shook her head and sighed. She turned and stormed angrily away, leaving Kevin wishing he hadn't reacted the way he had. He knew he should call her back and say sorry, but after years as a villain, he still hadn't quite got the hang of being nice to people.

Instead he turned his attention to Ben, who was still sitting on the cold stone kerb, still watching the hologram of his grandfather repeating the same message for about the thousandth time.

'You know, my dog used to gnaw on this spot on his butt over and over,' Kevin announced. 'The vet made us put a cone around his neck.'

At first, Ben didn't reply. He was focused completely on the image of his Grandpa Max as the recording came to an end once more.

'Easy does it,' he told Kevin, getting up from the kerb. 'I'm not the one you're mad at.'

'Cut me a break here,' Kevin pleaded. He needed something to take his mind off his row with Gwen. 'You want to go fight some aliens or something?'

'Or something,' Ben nodded. 'Let me see your Plumber's badge.'

Kevin reached into his pocket, dug out the shiny green and black badge and tossed it to Ben. At the flick of a switch a detailed map was projected into the air just a few centimetres above the badge's surface. At various points around the map, several small white dots blinked on and off.

'Each of these blips shows the location of another badge,' Ben explained.

Kevin shrugged. 'Yep.'

'And where there's a Plumber's badge, we'll find a Plumber,' continued Ben. 'Or at least a Plumber's kid.'

The map vanished back down into the badge, as Ben passed the device back to Kevin.

'C'mon,' Ben urged, hurrying around to the passenger door of Kevin's car. 'We're off, and you're driving.'

Kevin took a step towards the driver's door, then paused. He turned and looked towards Gwen, who was leaning against a nearby lamp post, her back to the boys.

'You coming?' Kevin asked.

Gwen raised her head, scowled at him, then crossed to the car and climbed into the back without saying a word.

Kevin's car roared along the fast lane of a busy motorway, its powerful headlights slicing easily through the dark.

Up front, Ben was studying the blips on the glowing green map. In the back, Gwen was still in a bad mood.

'Plumber. Plumber. Plumber, Plumber, Plumber,' she sang. 'You ever notice that if you say a word enough times it loses its meaning?' Gwen stared at Kevin. 'Like a chance to ask someone out. Every time that chance comes along it has less and less meaning, until you don't have the chance any more at all.'

In the driver's seat, Kevin rolled his eyes. 'Oh,' he mumbled, 'for crying out loud.'

On another stretch of the motorway, less than half a mile ahead, a schoolgirl named Trina was shuffling along the side of the road. Her dark skin was wrinkle-free, and her limbs still looked strong, but from the way she was stumbling there was obviously something very wrong.

She staggered into the first lane of the motorway, her legs barely able to support her. Trina didn't hear the blaring of the truck's horn. She didn't notice the squealing of brakes, or the cry of panic from the driver as he struggled to avoid smashing directly into her.

KAA-RAASH!

The truck toppled sideways as it turned, hitting the concrete hard. The vehicle's weight carried it onwards, metal screeching noisily as it scraped and sparked across the concrete.

BOOM!

With a sound like thunder, the truck crashed hard against the stone support pillar of the road bridge that crossed above this section of the motorway. The force of the crash shattered the pillar to dust. The sharp screams of terrified motorists split the night air, as the entire bridge began to crumble to pieces.

CHAPTER TWO

TEAMWORK IN ACTION

Kevin jammed his foot down hard on the brake, bringing the car to a halt less than a metre from a widening crack in the tarmac. They managed to stop just before the bridge, so they were safe. The same couldn't be said for the dozens of other cars that were slowly sliding towards the collapsing edge. It was a fifteen metre drop to the road below. No one inside those vehicles would survive the fall.

Ben, Gwen and Kevin leapt into action. In just a few seconds the whole bridge would collapse. There was no time to lose.

The man who had been driving the truck was stuck inside his cab. A fire had broken out and was spreading quickly along the length of the vehicle. The driver banged on the glass and shouted for help. As Kevin scrambled down the embankment to rescue him, Ben and Gwen turned their attention to the bridge itself.

One of the cars had begun sliding more quickly than the others. Ben gasped as he realised it was rolling right towards the side of the bridge. The whole structure was leaning sideways now, and there was nothing to stop the car plunging over the edge.

'Gwen!' Ben cried, but his cousin was already on to it. Twin beams of pink energy snaked from her hands. They streaked through the night, racing to get ahead of the sliding car.

Inside the vehicle, the driver and his family shut their eyes, holding on to each other tightly. They screamed as they felt the car tip, before realising they weren't falling nearly as quickly as they'd expected.

Opening his eyes, the driver peered outside. The car slid gently down a glowing slope of magical energy, before coming to a gentle rest in a safe area below.

A cloud of white dust billowed up from the bridge as more and more stone began to break away. Drivers and passengers swarmed from inside their cars, running frantically to try to get away.

KE-RRACK!

The concrete structure shook violently, sending a few of the runners stumbling towards the drop. Two more energy beams extended from Gwen's fingertips. They merged together, forming another long slope.

The fleeing people flashed Gwen a grateful smile as they leapt one-by-one on to the slide and slipped down to the safety of the ground below.

There were too many of them, Ben knew. Too many people, and not enough time before the bridge gave way completely. There was no way they would all make it, unless . . .

Ben twisted the dial of the Omnitrix and the hologram of a hulking, dinosaur-like alien flashed up. With a slam he activated the alien watch, and a cloud of green energy swirled around him.

Ben felt his heart swell in his chest and his bones begin to grow. His skin stretched and grew thicker, as a row of spiky plates extended from his spine and the muscular tail that sprouted from beneath it.

In less than a second, Ben was gone. In his place stood the hulking Humungousaur!

The dinosaur alien bounded over the side of the bridge, his powerful feet cracking the concrete where he landed. The collapsing structure was several metres above him. Fortunately, that wasn't a problem.

All around the motorway, onlookers pointed and stared, as Humungousaur's already giant frame began to expand. Up and up he stretched, until his mighty shoulders were wedged tightly against the underside of the bridge.

The alien gritted his sharp teeth. The weight of the bridge with all those cars on top was almost unbearable. Even with his incredible strength, he wouldn't be able to support it for long.

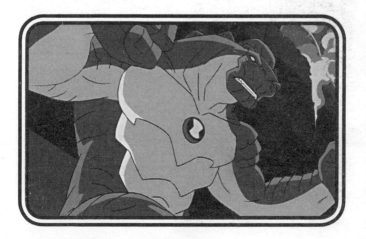

'Get everyone down,' he barked at Gwen. 'I can't hold this together much longer.'

Gwen was working as fast as she could, but there were at least twenty people still waiting to slide to safety. She glanced nervously down at the road below. Kevin was there, pulling the truck driver free from his burning cab. Another life saved. Only the people on the bridge were in danger now.

And then Gwen saw her – the shambling shape of Trina, still wandering aimlessly across the road. A car was speeding towards her, the driver too distracted by the events on the bridge to see what was directly in his path.

'The girl!' Gwen cried.

Kevin looked up and spotted Trina. He was too far away. He couldn't reach her in time. 'Ben!' he bellowed, desperately.

Humungousaur could see what was happening, but if he moved from the bridge it would surely collapse, killing all those still

stranded on it. 'Hands . . . full,' he managed
to growl.

At last the driver of the car saw Trina
standing in front of him, but he was too late.
She was too close by the time he spotted her.
There was no way he could avoid knocking
her down.

Suddenly, a streak of yellow light tore
down from the sky. The strong arms of a
glowing, golden figure wrapped around Trina's
waist, before they both launched skywards, out
of the path of the speeding car.

Gwen watched the scene unfold, her eyes wide with wonder. She was so fixed on the shimmering outline of Trina's rescuer that she barely noticed the last few people had already slid down to safety.

'Everyone's OK,' she announced, finally. The power-beam escape slide fizzled out, and Gwen floated down to join Kevin.

With a grunt, Humungousaur let the bridge go. It collapsed instantly, sending huge chunks of shattered stone raining down on the now empty truck.

One quick flash of green later, and the enormous alien became the considerably less gigantic Ben. He rushed over to join Gwen and Kevin, and all three of them watched the mysterious hero drift back to Earth, still carrying Trina in his arms.

As his feet touched the ground, the golden
outline faded, revealing a blonde-haired, blue-
eyed boy of around Ben's age. He had a square
jaw and was smartly dressed, like a lead actor
in an old adventure movie.

Trina jolted awake as he sat her on the
pavement. 'I – I have to get out of here,' she
wailed. 'I was running, and I . . . I . . .'

'It's OK, Trina,' the boy assured her.
'You're safe now.'

A whimper escaped Trina's lips, but she
seemed to relax a little. Her rescuer looked up at

Ben, Gwen and Kevin who stood next to him.

'Whoever you guys are, whatever you are, thanks,' he said. His eyes flicked back to Trina. 'Something strange has been happening to the girls at our school lately.'

'Glad to help. We made a good team out there,' replied Ben, before a familiar green and black logo on the boy's belt caught his eye. 'You've got a Plumber's badge,' he gasped.

'Yeah, my dad gave it to me,' said the blonde-haired boy. 'You guys know about the Plumbers?'

Kevin pulled his own badge from his pocket and held it up. 'At this point, we may as well be them.'

'I'm Ben Tennyson. This is Kevin and my cousin, Gwen.'

The boy's eyes grew wide. 'Wait. Ben Tennyson?' he asked. 'I'm a huge fan of yours. But I heard you disappeared.' He stood up and took hold of Ben's hand, shaking it firmly. 'My name is Mike Morningstar.'

Morningstar shook Kevin's hand, too, before moving on to Gwen. As their hands touched, a spark of yellow electricity fizzled between their palms.

'Oh!' Gwen gasped.

'Wow,' said Morningstar. 'That's never happened before.'

'Maybe it's because we both have powers,' suggested Gwen.

Morningstar smiled. 'That's a theory.'

'Anyway,' coughed Kevin, stepping between the pair, 'now that we've all met?'

Morningstar managed to tear his eyes away from Gwen's.

'I should make sure Trina gets home OK,' he announced. 'But after that, why don't we meet up at my place and talk?'

'Sure,' said Ben.

'Sounds good,' agreed Gwen.

Kevin groaned. 'Can't wait.'

With a final nod, Morningstar scooped Trina up in his arms and leapt up into the sky. The golden glow surrounded him in an instant, covering him, Trina, and the circle-shaped marking that appeared to be burned on to Trina's forearm.

A marking that looked a lot like a round mouth full of very sharp teeth.

CHAPTER THREE

A ZOMBIE PLAGUE

morningstar's 'place' turned out to be a plush apartment in the grounds of his family's stately home. The expensive carpet padded softly beneath their feet as Ben, Gwen and Kevin followed Morningstar inside.

'Mum and her new husband live in the main house,' Morningstar explained. 'They leave me alone. Let me do what I want.'

'Cool,' whistled Ben.

Morningstar opened the door and stepped back, motioning for Gwen to go through. 'After you,' he smiled.

Gwen gave Kevin a brief smirk, then stepped through the doorway. Ben followed, with Morningstar a step behind. Before Kevin could follow them, the door swung shut on his face with a hard slam.

Kevin pushed open the door and stormed through, rubbing his nose where the door had hit it, and muttering below his breath. 'Nice.'

The room they had entered was bigger than Ben's whole house. Banks of computers and other high-tech gadgets covered almost every surface. Tiny lights blinked and flashed on them, like a thousand distant stars.

'What is all this stuff?' asked Ben.

'Some of my dad's Plumber gear. I brought it over from his headquarters.' Morningstar turned to Gwen. 'I could take you there later if you want.'

'We'd all like to see it,' enthused Ben.

'It'd make my day for sure,' Kevin scowled, sarcastically.

Morningstar's gaze was still fixed on Gwen. 'Here,' he said, taking her by the hand, 'let me show you something.'

They walked across to where a giant

monitor covered a large section of wall. On screen was a series of complicated-looking maps, diagrams and symbols.

'I'm patched into the central Plumbers' monitoring network,' Morningstar explained. 'It's connected to everything. Global and interplanetary internet. Earthbound law enforcement frequencies. Oh, and of course the badge communicator channel.'

Kevin and Ben glanced at each other, then down at Kevin's badge. 'Communicator channel?' Kevin asked.

Morningstar raised one eyebrow. 'Yeah. You did know the badges are communicators, didn't you?'

'So,' said Gwen, before the boys could admit they didn't, 'you keep an eye on things with this stuff and use your powers to help people. You're like your neighbourhood's very own superhero.'

'Never thought of it that way,'

Morningstar replied, 'but I guess so.'

Ben had been watching the boy closely, and he was impressed by what he saw. He nodded as he came to a decision.

'You know that I'm thinking?' he said.

'I know what I'm thinking,' mumbled Kevin, too quietly for anyone to hear.

'You should come and join our team,' suggested Ben.

'Don't you think we should, I don't know, get to know this guy a little more?' asked Kevin.

'What's to know? He's got the powers, he's got the gear. And it's what Grandpa told us to do.'

Kevin began to protest, but Ben stepped away and continued talking to Morningstar. 'My Grandpa Max was a Plumber, and he disappeared while looking into this big alien conspiracy that's going on against Earth. We're trying to find him so we can stop it. Do you want to help us?'

Morningstar's eyes flicked across to Gwen. 'I'd love to,' he said with a smile.

Without warning the lights in the apartment began to flicker and dim. Some of the computer monitors went dark, but the main terminal managed to remain on.

Then, as suddenly as it had started, the electricity problem stopped, and full power was restored to the room.

'Perhaps you forgot to pay your electric bill?' sneered Kevin.

'The electricity's been a little unreliable lately. No worries, my backup generator has kicked in.'

'This isn't a black-out,' said Ben. He was staring up at the big computer screen. 'Look at this spike in power usage at the local power substation. The energy drain is enormous.'

'Really?' frowned Morningstar.

'You said that something strange was happening in town,' Ben continued.

'And this definitely qualifies.'

'If you need to check it out, we'll help,' volunteered Gwen.

'Thanks,' Morningstar nodded. 'Well, perhaps we should go to the substation now.'

All four of them made for the door, Morningstar leading the way. Halfway to the exit, something on her wrist caught Gwen's eye. A quiet cry of shock caught in her throat as she looked down and realised a strange, circular pattern had begun to form on her skin, just like the one she'd noticed on Trina's.

She pulled her sleeve lower, covering up the mark. She could worry about it later. Right now, there was a mystery to solve.

The low, squat buildings of the electrical substation were in near-darkness when Ben and the others approached the gate. A steady high-voltage hum was the only indication that the station was even up and running.

A padlock and chain lay on the ground beside the fence. Ben nudged the gate and it swung open without a sound.

'Stay sharp,' Ben whispered, sneaking through the open gate. 'We've got company.'

The electrical hum seemed to grow louder and louder as the group crept stealthily across the grounds of the substation. Morningstar glanced up at one of the tall pylons that loomed high overhead.

'Sounds like that weird buzzing sound you always hear in old monster movies,' he whispered.

Ben gulped, stopped abruptly and pointed ahead. Before them, the withered, zombie-like outline of a girl stood between two pylons, her bony arms stretched above her. Tendrils of electricity crackled from the metal posts.

They wrapped around the girl. Her eyes glowed an eerie shade of white as she absorbed the energy into her body.

With a sudden start, the girl realised she was being watched. She ducked sideways and tore a large piece of machinery from the base of the pylon, lifting it easily over her head.

With a hiss of animal rage, the zombie girl hurled the machinery towards the group. Gwen threw up her hands. A shield of magical energy surrounded them, deflecting the projectile at the last second.

With a low moan, another girl shambled from the shadows beside them. Her frail arms were outstretched, her lifeless eyes staring blankly. Another girl emerged behind her, then another, and another, until the heroes found themselves facing an entire horde of zombies.

'The girls here?' said Ben, nervously. 'Kinda weird.'

'They're wearing uniforms from my school,' Morningstar said. 'But I don't recognise any of them.'

One of the zombies ripped a metal post clean out of the ground. She advanced again, swinging the steel pole like a baseball bat.

Stepping protectively in front of Gwen, Morningstar raised his clenched fists. Twin bands of golden power exploded from them. The beams struck the ground in front of the approaching zombies, forcing them backwards a few paces.

'Energy bolts,' cried Ben. 'Nice.'

'Try not to hurt them,' Morningstar urged. 'Maybe we can reverse this. Whatever it is.'

'Try not to hurt them?' snorted Kevin, as the pole-wielding zombie lunged at him, snarling angrily. He ducked the clumsy swing and rolled sideways to where another post jutted up from the ground.

Pressing his fingers against the metal, Kevin began to absorb its properties. His body took on the strength and appearance of polished steel. If these ladies wanted a fight, then he would be only too happy to give them one.

Ben stumbled backwards, struggling against the choke-hold of another zombie girl. His back slammed hard against a thick metal cabinet marked 'High Voltage' and he yelped with pain.

The girl released her grip, but quickly swung with a wild punch. Ben twisted to the side, barely avoiding the blow. He watched, amazed, as the girl's tiny fist drove a hole straight through the metal door.

The zombie screeched with inhuman rage as she pulled her hand free. The entire door tore away, and Ben realised the girl was now holding on to a thick electrical wire. Blue sparks, like mini lightning bolts, fizzled at the damaged end of the cable.

The girl began to advance once more, stabbing at him with the crackling cable. If it touched him he was done for. There was nothing else for it. Ben slammed the control dial of the Omnitrix.

It was hero time.

CHAPTER FOUR

A DESPERATE BATTLE

CLANG! The metal pole bounced harmlessly off Kevin's steel body. Moving quickly, Kevin threw a punch, lifting her off her feet, then dropping her to the ground. It should have been more than enough to knock her out, but somehow the girl got back up.

A flash of green caught his attention. Kevin glanced across to where Ben had been. A tall, purple and blue figure stood there, facing off against another of the zombies. Ben had transformed into the rock-bodied, crystal-formed ChromaStone.

With a roar, the zombie girl threw herself at the alien, jabbing the electrical cable into his chest. A lightning storm seemed to whip up around ChromaStone, buzzing and zapping across his stony surface.

'That's not going to work,' ChromaStone grinned. 'I'm a conductor.'

He extended a finger and pressed it against the girl's head. The electrical current passed harmlessly through his body and flowed into hers. As soon as the bright blue sparks touched her, the zombie screamed and toppled backwards on to the ground.

ChromaStone smiled, lifted his finger, and blew away the thin line of grey smoke that curled up from the tip.

A series of bright yellow streaks screamed down from above, striking the ground and throwing rock and debris in all directions. Morningstar was airborne, blasting at the ground, doing everything he could to drive the zombies back without hurting them.

Gwen's fingers danced, sending tendrils of pink energy snaking towards a few of the zombie girls. Like ropes, the energy trails wrapped around the girls, tying them tightly together. They struggled against their bonds, but Gwen was too strong.

Or was she?

A flicker of pain flitted across Gwen's face as the effort of using her powers suddenly became too much. The pink bands that held the zombies in place faded to black, before shattering like brittle glass.

Suddenly the world was spinning and Gwen was falling, too weak to even stand. A split second before her head hit the ground, a familiar golden figure caught her.

'Are you all right?' Morningstar asked.

'I . . . I don't know. I felt weak for a second,' Gwen stammered, struggling back upright. She looked up at Morningstar and smiled. 'I feel better now.'

Morningstar returned her smile. 'Here, hold my hand,' he said. 'Use my energy.'

The moment their hands met,

Morningstar's glittering golden glow began to surround Gwen. His power recharged her, allowing her to project an energy shield and drive the approaching zombies back.

With the girls pushed back, Morningstar unleashed some power bolts at a nearby pylon. The tall metal structure folded in on itself like a house of cards. It crashed to the ground, forming a barrier between the zombies and the heroes.

Realising there was no possible way through, the zombie girls growled angrily, then turned and fled back into the shadows from where they came.

'Ah, nice going,' snapped Kevin, returning to his normal form. 'They are all getting away!'

'Sorry,' said Morningstar.

With a flurry of green energy, ChromaStone transformed back into Ben. He rested a hand on Morningstar's shoulder.

'It's OK. We all make mistakes,' he said, reassuringly. 'The important thing is we stopped them from . . . Uh, doing whatever it is they were doing. We'll get better as we work together more.'

Morningstar turned and stared deeply into Gwen's eyes. 'We do make a good team,' he smiled.

Gwen blushed slightly. 'Uh-huh.'

'What happened just now?' Kevin asked Gwen, trying to interrupt. 'You looked like you were gonna faint.'

Ignoring Kevin, Gwen smiled shyly up at Morningstar. 'I can't thank you enough for helping me.'

'You could if you had dinner with me.'

'Right now?' Gwen asked.

'I'm hungry. How about you?'

Gwen wrapped her arm around Morningstar's. 'I was just going to suggest the same thing.'

'OK, what is up with you?' Kevin demanded. 'You've been ignoring me ever since we got here, you were lousy in the fight and now you're just acting goofy.'

'Why are you pretending to care?' Gwen sneered, as she and Morningstar began to walk away. 'Later.'

Kevin watched them go, barely able to contain his anger. He spun to face Ben. 'You just gonna stand there?'

'No,' Ben replied. 'I was going to go sit in the car.'

'I don't trust this guy,' said Kevin, following Ben towards the car park. 'And I don't think you should have been so quick to make him one of the team.'

'Admit it, you're just jealous because Gwen likes him.'

Kevin opened his mouth to argue, before an idea suddenly struck him.

'You know what?' he said with a sly grin. 'It's fine.'

One fast car journey later, and Ben and Kevin were standing outside the door of Morningstar's apartment. Kevin had used his absorbing abilities to turn his fingers to metal, and now had one jammed into the door's heavy lock. He wiggled the finger around inside the keyhole, listening for a click.

'This is why you changed your mind about Mike going off with Gwen?' Ben sighed. 'So we could spy on him?'

'Yeah,' Kevin smirked.

'Well, stop!'

'He ain't right, Ben,' Kevin insisted. 'If you're not gonna check him out, I am.'

'You're doing the wrong thing, Kevin. The old Kevin thing. Step away from the door.'

'You really want to fight me over some new guy?' Kevin asked. 'That's how you're gonna build a team?'

The lock mechanism gave a faint click and Kevin edged the door open. He smiled, pleased at himself. 'And they said I didn't learn anything in the Null Void.'

Before Kevin could step inside, both boys heard a familiar voice.

'Is Mike home?' asked Trina. She was shuffling up the path, her whole body shaking. 'He hasn't called me back since you and that new girl showed up.'

'Trina, right? Yeah, Morningstar ain't here right now,' Kevin replied. He realised she was looking at the open door. He had to think fast. 'We're . . . just picking up some stuff for him.'

'Then you know where he is!' Trina cried. 'Can you take me?'

'No,' said Ben. 'I mean, he's busy.'

Trina let out a soft sob of despair. 'I need to see him. Why won't he see me?'

Kevin studied the girl. She looked frail and weak – even worse than she'd looked at the motorway. His eyes fell to her trembling arms and he realised they were covered in dark, circular tattoos.

'Where'd you get those marks on your arms?' he asked. When the girl didn't answer, Kevin turned to Ben. 'I saw those same marks on that zombie girl that tried to tenderise me.'

'I just wanna see Mike,' Trina wept.

'Yeah, I'm getting that,' Kevin nodded.

'Call me crazy,' he told Ben, 'but do you think it's possible that Morningstar's the one making the girls this way?'

Ben blinked. 'You're crazy.'

'Look, it didn't really hit me 'til just now,' Kevin continued, 'but I've noticed that Gwen's been wearing her sleeves lower than usual. She's hiding something.'

'You're saying Gwen has marks like that on her arms?'

'I haven't seen them for sure,' admitted Kevin, 'but it makes sense.'

Ben rubbed his chin, thoughtfully. 'Come to think of it, Trina was all weak and wobbly when we first saw her on the motorway. Gwen was the same way at the power plant. It's possible that Gwen might have caught whatever bug is doing this.'

'Yeah,' said Kevin, his eyes narrowing to slits. 'And the bug's name is Mike Morningstar.'

CHAPTER FIVE

THE FINAL CONFRONTATION

Smoke billowed from the tyres of Kevin's car as it screeched around a sharp bend in the road. Inside, Kevin pushed the accelerator pedal to the floor, powering the vehicle through the turn.

'Fact is you've been against Morningstar since the minute we met him,' Ben said. 'Because Gwen likes him more than she likes you.'

'Yeah, some of that,' Kevin said with a shrug. 'But now Gwen's in trouble, and you're too stuck on following your Grandpa's instructions to see it.'

Kevin spun the car around yet another corner, bouncing Ben around in the front passenger seat.

'Well, if Mike's turning those girls into creatures, why isn't Trina one?' Ben asked.

'I don't know. Maybe it's like a vampire thing. Maybe it takes a while before they go all zombie.'

'Even if you're right, we don't know where they went for dinner,' Ben pointed out. 'How are we supposed to find her?'

'Easy,' grinned Kevin, pulling out his Plumber's badge and activating the holo-map. 'We find him.'

Inside the abandoned bunker that had once been his father's secret headquarters, Morningstar was gripping Gwen tightly by her arms. Gwen looked barely conscious. Her skin was turning grey and wrinkled, as the life force was sucked out of her by the strange round

mouths that had appeared in the middle of
Morningstar's palms.

'Your energy is like nothing I've ever felt
before. When it flows into me, I feel invincible!'
Morningstar licked his lips, enjoying the taste of
the power. 'From the moment I touched you,
I knew I'd found the only girl I'd ever need.'

With a splintering of wood, the front door
of the building exploded inwards and Kevin and
Ben charged through. They stared in horror and
shock as they realised Kevin's suspicions had

been right all along.

'Gwen!' Kevin cried. He and Ben sprinted forwards, but a blast of yellow energy scorched the air around them. One of the bolts suddenly slammed into Ben's chest, sending him tumbling backwards.

Pressing his hands against the concrete floor, Kevin absorbed its strength. His body now rock-solid, he resumed his charge towards Morningstar and the helpless Gwen. 'Get away from her,' he roared.

Another sudden and powerful blast slammed into Kevin. Even in rock form he wasn't strong enough to deflect it. In a cloud of stone-dust he thudded hard against the back wall of the bunker.

Still dazed, Ben struggled to activate the Omnitrix. Gwen was lying on the floor now, barely moving. She didn't have much time left.

At last, Ben's fingers found the control dial. He pressed it down and sighed with relief, as the familiar swirl of green energy wrapped around him.

'Jet Ray!' he cried, launching his now bright-red alien form into the air. Jet Ray's mighty wings flapped twice, circling him around to face his target. The alien unleashed the full fury of his neuroshock laser blasts on Morningstar, but they had no effect.

'Go away!' Morningstar roared. He fired a devastating energy-bolt that struck the flying alien hard. With a groan, Jet Ray plunged to the ground. By the time he struck the concrete, he had already turned back into Ben.

Morningstar's eyes blazed. 'Gwen's mine now.'

Kevin had something to say about that. He sprinted forwards and hurled himself at the glowing figure, knocking him to the floor. A concrete fist slammed into Morningstar's jaw and he hissed in pain.

Before Kevin could land another punch, a blast of yellow light sent him backflipping off the fallen villain. The blow was so powerful it shattered the stone shell surrounding Kevin, stripping it away and turning him back into flesh and bone.

'You're out of your league,' Morningstar sneered. 'All I ever wanted was power and then you brought me Gwen.'

Ben tried to get to his feet, but he hadn't recovered from Morningstar's blast. From the shadows he spotted the shuffling shapes of the zombie girls they'd fought at the power station. They were advancing slowly, shambling towards the fallen heroes.

'I guess I should thank you,' Morningstar said. His eyes flicked up to the ceiling, where a huge air-conditioning pipe hung above Ben and Kevin. The villain smiled and raised his hands. 'I know the perfect thing.'

Still grinning, Morningstar unleashed a power bolt. It screamed through the air, on a direct collision course with the heavy length of metal pipe.

Just before it brought the whole thing crashing down, the energy blast fizzled and faded. Morningstar frowned, then looked down to where a withered hand was clutching one of his feet.

It took all her remaining strength, but Gwen pulled herself up. She held Morningstar's arms, and the air around her shimmered as she began to take her life force back.

'What are you doing?' Morningstar cried.

'Coming to my senses,' Gwen replied.
The energy flowed into her, faster and faster.
In seconds her withered frame was back to
normal, her skin no longer grey.

'Stop this!' pleaded Morningstar, but it
was too late. He screamed as the last of the
energy he had stolen from Gwen left his body.
Gwen released her grip, leaving Morningstar to
slump to the floor.

'Kevin!' she cried, running over to where
the two boys were still lying.

'Girls,' barked Morningstar, motioning to

the zombies. 'Come here to me.'

Moaning softly, the girls turned and shuffled towards the energy thief. 'Give me your power,' he ordered them. 'Help me. Feed me.'

The girls shuffled closer. There would be feeding done, but Morningstar wouldn't be the one to do it. He screamed once again as the zombie girls all took hold of him, sucking their energy back into their withered bones.

In a few moments it was all over. Gasping for breath, Morningstar lay motionless on the floor. Around him, the girls who had been his victims sneered down in disgust. They were back to normal now, and they would never fall for his tricks again.

Kevin reached down and plucked the Plumber's badge from Morningstar's belt. 'You don't deserve this,' he said.

And with that, Kevin crushed the badge into dust.

Kevin drove them away from the bunker.

'I'm sorry I took Morningstar's side over yours,' Ben said to Kevin. He turned to Gwen. 'And that I wasn't watching your back.'

'It wasn't your fault,' Gwen replied. 'Morningstar had some kind of control over me.'

'It was my fault,' Ben insisted. 'I was in such a hurry to build our team, I ignored the danger. If I'm going to be a good leader, I'm going to need to show better judgement.'

'If you're gonna be a good leader, you need to stop sounding like such a fool,' Kevin suggested.

A wicked smile spread across Ben's face. 'So Kevin,' he asked. 'When are you gonna ask Gwen out?'

Oh great, thought Kevin. Here we go again!

CHAPTER ONE

SANTA MIRA

The rain came down in sheets, rattling like gunfire on the tin metal roof of the Cozy Cup Diner. A figure stood there in the cold, wet night, his eyes locked on the coffee shop's steamed-up window.

Icy drops of rain trickled down beneath the collar of the man's coat, making him shiver.

He pulled the coat tighter around him, adjusted the brim of his hat, and set off towards the front door of the diner.

A bell above the door gave a merry jingle as the man stepped inside. Over by the counter, a grey-haired waitress looked up at her customer. The badge on her uniform said 'Edna'. Other than the man, she was the only person in the place.

Edna's gaze followed the new arrival as he crossed to a booth and squeezed his plump frame into a seat behind the table.

A dirty menu was shoved in front of him. 'Like to hear about the special?'

'Just coffee,' the mysterious man replied.

'Don't get many strangers here,' Edna said. 'What brings you to Santa Mira?'

'Great fishing. Great weather.'

Edna looked out of the window as a flash of lightning cracked the sky. 'Our fish are all farm raised. And this is the rainy season.'

The man slipped his hat off, revealing a head of neatly cropped grey hair. Grandpa Max smiled at the waitress.

'I was misinformed,' he said.

With a shrug, Edna slipped a plate on to the table in front of him. It was covered by a grubby metal lid. 'Here's your special.'

Max glanced down at the plate. 'I didn't order that,' he said.

'It's on the house,' Edna smirked, lifting the lid off the plate.

A purple octopus-like alien sprung forwards, its teeth chomping hungrily. Max's Plumber instincts kicked in and he managed to knock the alien away. He recognised the creature as a Xenocyte – nasty critters with six legs, one eye and a brain that bulged unpleasantly on the top of their bodies.

A pair of strong arms grabbed him from behind. Max snapped his head backwards, against Edna's nose. Unharmed, the waitress didn't even flinch.

'You're one strong lady,' said Max. 'Or are you?'

Reaching behind him, Max caught hold of Edna's hair and pulled. Her skin came away in his hand, revealing the bulging, bug-eye of a DNAlien.

'DNAlien' was the nickname given to the minions of the HighBreed, an evil alien race bent on total world domination. The DNAliens had once been human, until Xenocytes had merged with them, turning their bodies into little more than mindless drones for the HighBreed to control.

Max lifted his feet and placed them against the side of the table. With a grunt he shoved backwards, sending both him and the DNAlien crashing into the table directly behind.

CRRAASH!

The DNAlien hit the tabletop first. The force of Grandpa's push made the table snap in two as the creature fell to the floor. Max rolled sideways to safety, fighting for breath. He had knocked one alien out, but he was far from out of danger.

The Xenocyte screeched as it scuttled across the floor towards him. If it managed to clamp on to his head it would begin bonding with him. Then he would be completely under the HighBreeds' control.

Grandpa reached up and snatched a heavy coffee pot from the diner counter. With a roar he brought the hot, metal container smashing down. The Xenocyte's squidgy body burst with a sickening squelch.

Another bolt of lightning flashed across the sky as Grandpa Max got shakily to his feet. He looked down at the fallen aliens and sneered. 'I said "just coffee".'

'Uh . . . no,' scowled Kevin, polishing the bonnet of his car. 'Or let me put it another way.' He glanced up at Ben. 'No.'

'Come on, Kevin, he's my cousin,' Ben pleaded. Kevin had been cleaning his car for hours, and Ben had been arguing with him almost as long. 'He was supposed to be home from college two days ago.'

'And you want me to waste my time driving around, looking for your cousin?'

'I know how it sounds,' Ben replied. 'The police said to wait. I'm sure he's fine, we just don't know where he is.'

'Daytona Beach or Fort Lauderdale,' Kevin shrugged, his attention still fixed on his car. The polished metal gleamed in the light of the full moon. 'He's a college student.'

'No. He called from the road and said his car broke down in some town called Santa Mira,' Ben told him. 'We haven't heard anything since. His folks are worried.'

'And I'm supposed to care why?'

'Because he's my brother,' said a voice from nearby. Kevin looked up and saw Gwen. Her skin was pale and her eyes were puffy, like she'd been crying. She looked scared.

Kevin sighed and straightened himself up. 'Get in.'

It was a long way to Santa Mira, and it was almost midnight by the time they turned off the main road and pulled into the town. The rain battered down so hard the car's windscreen wipers were barely able to keep up.

'You're really sweet to do this, Kevin. Ken is – '

'What?' Kevin laughed. 'Ken? Your brother's name is Ken? Gwen and Ken Tennyson? What're your folks' names, Sven and

Jen?' He glanced in his rear view mirror and grinned. 'I'm talking to you, Ben.'

'Yes. Our names rhyme and you noticed,' Ben replied. 'Good for you.'

'Just having some fun, man,' said Kevin. 'I don't see what the big deal is.'

'Ken took Ben to his first soccer game,' explained Gwen, softly. 'When his band played, he snuck me and my friends backstage.' She bit her lip as she stared through the window at the rain. 'Ken's the coolest guy in the world.'

Kevin nodded towards the run-down, deserted buildings that lined the streets of Santa Mira. 'For a guy who's so cool, he sure picked a lame spot for a holiday.'

'Ken is totally cool,' Gwen said, defensively, 'and he didn't choose where the Awesome-mobile broke down.'

Kevin almost choked on his own laughter. 'The "Awesome-mobile"?'

'It's his car,' Ben explained.

'I told you, he's cool.'

'Oh, yeah,' Kevin sniggered. 'Who could doubt it?'

'I say we hit the garages in town,' Ben suggested. 'Find Ken's car, find Ken.'

'Good idea,' agreed Kevin. 'I mean, how many garages can this one horse town support, do you think?'

'Five,' Kevin groaned. 'Five garages.'

'Five garages so far,' corrected Ben. They were standing outside the fifth garage they had come across. Like the other four, it was locked up for the night. Ben had his face almost pressed against a grubby window, trying to see inside.

'And if the Awesome-mobile isn't in this one,' he said, 'we'll have to keep . . . bingo!'

Kevin pushed him out of the way, suddenly interested. 'You found a bingo game?'

'I found his car,' said Ben, pointing towards the far corner of the garage.

Narrowing his eyes, Kevin peered into the near-darkness. There, lurking in the corner, was the sorriest excuse for a car he had ever seen. Every part of it seemed to be either rusting, held in place by sticky tape, or both.

'That's the Awesome-mobile? That thing makes the Rustbucket look like a Ferrari.'

Gwen stepped back from the garage, looking around for anything that would tell them what time it would reopen the next day.

Just as she spotted the list of opening times, Kevin drove his shoulder hard against the door. There was a short, sharp snap of wood, and the door swung open.

Gwen scowled. 'Kevin!'

'Don't worry,' Kevin smiled, 'Ken is so cool he'll be happy to pay for that.'

Sneaking inside the garage, the three heroes began searching around and inside the car. Kevin wrinkled his nose in disgust when he opened a bulging grey sack that was sitting on the front seat.

'Dirty laundry for Mum to wash,' he said, half-choking. 'This guy really is a class act.'

'There must be a clue in here to help us find Ken,' Gwen said.

Ben lifted the car's bonnet. He peered down at the oil-stained engine, not sure what he was looking for.

'Whoa, what do we have here?' muttered Kevin, appearing behind Ben. He reached into the engine bay and detached a small silver object no larger than a matchbox.

'What is it?' Ben asked.

'The only thing in here not covered in rust. It's alien tech. Projects a field that dampens internal combustion.'

'His car was sabotaged?' Gwen gasped.

'Why? Ken's – '

'Too cool?'

'Too normal,' corrected Ben. 'He doesn't know anything about the aliens. Why would they go after him?'

As Kevin bent down to examine the engine more closely, Gwen leaned on the side of the car. Her hand touched something cold and slimy and she quickly pulled it away.

'Gross,' she frowned, examining the sticky yellow ooze that trickled along her fingers. 'What is this?'

'I don't know,' said Ben. He held up his watch. A bright green light was blinking furiously on its display. 'But the Omnitrix doesn't like it.'

'What's going on here?' mumbled Gwen.

A sound to their left caught their attention. All three of them spun on the spot and were surprised to find themselves facing two angry-looking men.

The larger of the two spat on the garage floor as he eyed the three heroes. 'Well now,' he said, menacingly. 'Wouldn't mind knowing that myself.'

CHAPTER TWO

SLIMEBALLS

The man was wearing mechanic's overalls and dirty gloves. Long strands of greasy hair poked out from beneath his filthy baseball cap. 'What are you lot doing in my garage?' he demanded.

The other man was carrying a large plastic cooler box. He sat it down on the ground before scurrying up to join his friend. He was dressed almost identically to the first man, but his eyes were darker and narrower.

'You want me to call the sheriff, Moe?' he asked, revealing a mouth full of rotten teeth.

Ben spotted the name tag on the man's overalls. 'Yeah, you do that, Shem,' he suggested. 'I bet they'd be real interested to find out what happened to the kid who owns this car.'

'Whaddaya mean?' drawled Moe. 'How should we know? He dropped off the car, we fixed it, he didn't come back.'

Kevin reached in through the car's window and turned the key. The engine spluttered once, made a sound like grinding metal, then died.

'You fixed it, huh?'

Unseen by any of them, Gwen had crept around behind Moe and Shem. She knelt down beside the cooler box and carefully prised open the lid. A thin layer of yellow goo lined the inside of the box.

'More slime,' she said, pulling away quickly in disgust.

'OK, that's it,' Ben snapped, approaching the mechanics. 'What is that stuff anyway? What was in there?'

Before the men could reply, a bolt of lightning lit up the night. The electrical surge made both men's skin flicker and become see-through, revealing strange and hideous alien shapes underneath.

'Check it out,' said Kevin. It's the DNA Hillbillies.'

Suddenly, Moe's throat began to swell and bulge. He opened his mouth and retched like he was about to be sick. Instead he coughed up a huge blob of yellow goo. It caught Gwen by surprise, splattering into her and pinning her against the garage wall.

Ben twisted the dial of the Omnitrix, but another ball of flying ooze swiftly encased him,

and he, too, found himself stuck to the wall like a fly to flypaper. He managed to lift his head in time to see Kevin trapped the same way.

Moe and Shem reached up and caught hold of their own faces. With a yank, the fake skin fell away, and their holographic disguises fizzled out. The two DNAliens crept closer to the helpless heroes, their pin-sharp teeth snapping hungrily at the air.

Ben struggled against the smelly yellow ooze. It had already begun to dry. In a few moments it would be rock hard and there would be no possible way to escape. His arm ached as he heaved it across his body. He gritted his teeth against the pain until his fingers at last found the cool metal surface of the Omnitrix.

'Humungousaur!' he roared, as his body began to grow and change. The dino-alien's mighty muscles ripped easily through the yellow gloop. He turned on the DNAliens, his hot breath forming clouds of steam in the cold of the garage.

Meanwhile, Gwen had also come up with an escape plan. Thin blades of pink energy swirled out from her eyes. They moved quickly along her body, slicing away the ooze and allowing her to pull herself free.

Angrily, she held up a hand and blasted one of the DNAliens with her magic. Panicked, the other creature turned to run, before realising it was heading straight for the snarling Humungousaur. Spinning on the spot, the alien darted the other way, its single green eye staring nervously over its shoulder.

KA-LANG!

The alien let out a brief shriek of pain as its head smacked against the solid steel shape of Kevin.

'That's a work-related accident. You can sue,' Kevin smirked, gazing down at the motionless form of the unconscious DNAlien.

'We got 'em,' he announced. 'Now what?'

The rain continued to fall as Ben, Gwen and Kevin climbed out of the car and studied the outside of the Cozy Cup Diner. This was the place Ken had telephoned from. The last time anyone had ever heard from him.

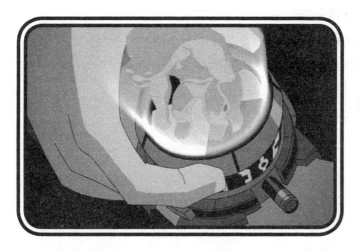

The coffee shop was closed. A quick

sweep of the area revealed nothing to indicate Ken had ever even been there. Gwen clenched her fists in frustration.

'I thought if we retraced Ken's steps we'd find a clue,' she said. 'But there's nothing here.'

THUD.

A delivery truck parked just around the corner from the coffee shop shook, as something inside it began to move. Ben and the others approached it, cautiously.

'I wouldn't say "nothing",' replied Ben.

Bracing themselves for what they might find, Ben rolled up the back door of the truck. A DNAlien wriggled around on the floor, its hands bound by glowing energy cuffs. A rag had been wedged into the creature's mouth to keep it quiet.

The DNAlien twisted, trying to get up. As it thrashed around, it toppled over a stack of cooler boxes, spilling yellow goo all over the floor. As the slime oozed closer, the Omnitrix began to flash and bleep wildly.

Kevin reached into the truck and snatched the rag from the DNAlien's mouth. Kevin was tired, cold and wet, and he needed someone to take his anger out on. 'Start talking,' he growled.

Still watching the Omnitrix, Ben brought it closer to the slime. The green light on the watch blinked faster, and the bleeping became a high-pitched alarm.

Then, as suddenly as it had started, the Omnitrix's strange behaviour stopped. A calm electronic voice emerged from somewhere within the watch.

'Unknown DNA sample acquired.'

Ben frowned. 'That's new.'

'Ben, you want to look at this,' said Gwen. She held up the rag that Kevin had pulled from the DNAlien's mouth. It was a scrap of a very familiar Hawaiian shirt.

'This is from his favourite shirt,' Ben quickly gasped.

'Whose favourite shirt?' asked Kevin.

'Grandpa Max's,' said Gwen. A pink glow crackled across her skin. With barely a twitch she wrapped the alien in powerful tendrils of magical energy. 'Tell us who tied you up,' she barked. 'Now!'

The DNAlien yelped as Gwen's energy bonds began to tighten around it. 'Max Tennyson,' the creature groaned. 'He wanted to find some kid.'

'Where is he?' demanded Gwen.

'I don't know,' winced the trapped alien. 'He cuffed me and left me here.'

'Not him. He can take care of himself,' said Gwen. 'The kid. Where is my brother?'

The tendrils were incredibly tight around the DNAlien now. Ben could see the brain on top of its head had started to bulge, as if it were about to pop. 'Hat – hatchery,' it managed to say. 'He's at the hatchery!'

'Look, I told you, I told you,' pleaded Ken. 'I have no idea where my grandfather is. I don't know anything!'

Ken struggled against the ropes that tied him to a heavy wooden chair. He'd been pulling against the bonds for hours, but all he'd done was hurt his wrists. He was well and truly trapped. Helpless. And with a hideous creature like nothing he'd ever seen before looming over him.

'I believe you,' hissed the DNAlien.

Ken allowed himself a sigh of relief. If the creature believed him, maybe it would let him go.

'Who – who are you?' he asked, in what he hoped was a friendly way.

'I'm glad you asked, Ken,' the DNAlien replied. 'I think the best way to get to know someone is to walk a mile in their shoes.'

The alien pulled the lid from a cooler box and reached inside. A Xenocyte wriggled as it was torn free from the yellow goo. The six-legged alien thrashed around excitedly as it was brought closer to Ken's face.

'What is that?' gasped Ken, horrified.

The DNAlien's mouth pulled into something like a grin. 'My shoes.'

With a disgusting **SCHLOP** the Xenocyte clamped on to the boy's face. Ken's scream echoed around the inside of the hatchery building, and out into the dark, rainy night.

CHAPTER THREE

ASSAULT ON THE HATCHERY

Kevin turned the ignition key and the engine of his car shuddered to a stop. The high, barbed-wire fence of the hatchery lay before them. Beyond it, the hatchery itself, and hopefully, Ken.

A man-sized hole had been burned through the wire mesh, providing the perfect way into the grounds of the hatchery.

Looks like someone got here before us, thought Ben, as all three of them hurried through the narrow gap. The rain lashed against them with every step, making it hard to see. They could make out three long, thin trenches cut into the ground. All three were filled with a murky green liquid, and seemed to lead all the way into the hatchery building.

'I'm cold,' complained Kevin, rubbing his arms. 'And wet.'

Ben pointed up towards a tall tower that rose high above the rest of the complex. 'Weather machine,' he said. 'The aliens are making it cold and rainy for whatever it is they're doing.'

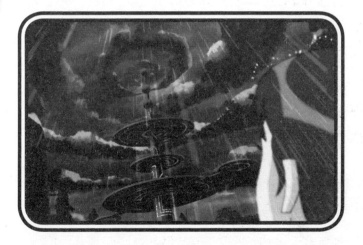

Gwen was squinting through the pouring rain, studying the main hatchery building. The entrance doors were closed. And there would almost certainly be guards standing right on the other side. They had a problem.

'How do we get in without being spotted?' she asked.

Ben thought for a moment, then peered down at one of the trenches that led into the building. It looked a bit like a long, narrow swimming pool. A long, narrow swimming pool filled to the brim with some disgusting, smelly green liquid.

Kevin guessed what was coming next. 'You gotta be kidding me,' he groaned. 'Who'd be crazy enough to swim in that?'

Deep inside the facility, a grey-haired head emerged from beneath a pool of the slimy green fluid. Grandpa Max wiped the gunk from around his eyes and studied his surroundings.

A complicated series of metal walkways

criss-crossed above him, leading to various doors dotted all around the room. Up on the left, a bulky shape leaned against a railing, its bulging green eye staring directly down at him. He'd been spotted!

The DNAlien sprinted across the walkway, its clawed hands making a grab for the button that would activate the alarm and bring reinforcements. It chattered excitedly to itself as it ran. Five metres away. Four. Three. It was going to make it!

THA-WACK!

The punch caught the alien hard on the side of the head, spinning it around just as Max let fly with another blow. This one knocked it flat on its back. The creature lay there for a moment, clutching its aching jaw. It was too dazed to react when Max pulled out the Null Void Projector gun. A beam of red energy flashed across the alien, before it was sucked into the emptiness of the Null Void.

Creeping through the closest door, Max found himself in a long, dark corridor. He ducked back around the corner before the two guards standing at the far end of the passageway could spot him.

Jamming his fingers in his mouth, Max gave a short whistle. He waited, body tensed, until he heard the clattering of the guards' footsteps racing along the corridor towards him.

Just as they drew level with the corner, Max lashed out. Two quick right hooks, a flash of the Null Projector, and both aliens were safely out of the way.

Staying alert in case of any more DNAlien activity, Max darted along the corridor. The thick metal door at the far end was electronically sealed, but it was nothing his Plumber's badge couldn't take care of. He swiped the device across the lock, and the door immediately swung open.

The glare of the lights in the room

dazzled Max as he stepped through the doorway. He blinked, adjusting to the sudden brightness, before spotting the shape lying slumped on the floor.

'Grandpa Max,' croaked the figure. 'Please help me.'

'Kenny. It's OK, boy,' said Max, reassuringly. He took Ken by the shoulder and tried to help him up. 'I'm here.'

As Ken turned, Max gave a strangled gasp of shock. A Xenocyte clung to his grandson's head, covering half his face. The one human eye Max could see seemed to plead with him as he hoisted Ken to his feet.

Suddenly, a shock of pain hit Max in the stomach. He tried to scream, but the electrical charge zapping through his body made his teeth clamp tightly together.

Max stumbled backwards. He saw the stun-gun in Ken's hand, and the grin which covered his half-alien face. And then he saw nothing but black, as he sank to the floor and slipped silently into unconsciousness.

Outside, Kevin was complaining. Again.

'Next time you ask me for a favour, remind me to say "no".'

'Don't be a baby,' snapped Gwen. 'My brother is in there, captured by DNAliens.'

They were trudging through the trench, chest-deep in the foul green liquid.

'At least he's dry,' Kevin moaned. 'And this stuff smells like – ' Something below the surface brushed against his leg, stopping him mid-sentence. 'What was that?'

All three of them scanned the surface of the water, none of them daring to make a move. The liquid rippled gently, but showed no other sign of movement.

Just before they decided it was a false alarm, a gloopy tentacle snaked up from the green fluid. In an instant it was around Gwen's neck. She barely had time to scream before it dragged her down into the murky depths of the trench.

The hatchery control centre looked like the surface of some strange alien planet. Long, stringy beams of solidified goo supported all manner of high-tech equipment. The walls, floor and ceiling were coated in a shiny red gunk. As Max was led into the room, his breath instantly formed clouds in the frosty air.

His two guards shoved him towards a raised control platform. Standing atop the platform was a towering alien, easily three metres tall. His skin was a ghostly shade of white, with four red eyes positioned just above his chest. Several more eyes covered the alien's otherwise featureless face. Max recognised the creature as a member of the HighBreed. He was probably the leader of all the DNAliens Max had encountered so far.

'Max Tennyson,' growled the HighBreed. 'You have been active in your retirement.'

Max stared up at the alien, unafraid. 'This is really just a hobby now,' he said with a shrug. 'Man my age has to stay active.'

'You have been a great irritation to us, vermin,' the HighBreed spat. 'You have delayed our plans.'

Grandpa Max nodded towards a stack of nearby cooler boxes. 'It's obvious you're producing these Xenocytes here,' he said.

'And that they somehow transform humans into these ugly freaks.'

'It can't be helped,' the alien replied. 'Their human half makes them repulsive.'

'All I want to know is why?'

'You will soon see for yourself, insect,' gloated the HighBreed. 'We are only a few hours away from completing the most crucial stage of the plan.'

'But why my grandson?' demanded Max. 'Why change Ken?'

'He was brought here as bait.' The HighBreed leaned down so his face was next to his prisoner's. 'With you out of the way, there is no one who can stop us!'

CHAPTER FOUR

INTO THE UNKNOWN

Ben's lungs burned as he lifted his head above the surface and gasped in some air. Kevin's head splashed up behind him, panic blazing behind his eyes.

'Where is she?' cried Ben.

'I can't see a thing down there!'

They ducked down below the surface, flailing their arms out, searching for any sign of Gwen. Precious seconds flowed by, until they couldn't hold their breath any longer.

They bobbed up and both gulped down a lungful of oxygen.

'Keep trying,' yelled Ben, but before they could dive again a pink glow lit up the water.

WHOOSH!

The glow exploded upwards, sending dozens of Xenocytes spiralling into the night sky. Gwen emerged from below the rippling surface. On either side of the trenches, Xenocytes plummeted to the ground with a series of slimy splats.

'Disgusting.' Gwen shuddered.

'It's about to get much worse,' warned Ben. He pointed to where the liquid flowed inside the hatchery building. The gap was narrow, and they would have to swim a long distance underwater to get to it.

Kevin shook his head. 'Oh, you're not saying – ' He watched Ben and Gwen take a breath and dive below the surface. Kevin sighed. 'Proving my point about this being the worst road trip ever!'

The trench became gradually deeper
as it entered the main part of the complex.
Although the water was dark and murky,
Ben could make out the squirming shapes of
hundreds of Xenocytes on the floor below. They
crawled from inside large round pods, which
Ben guessed must be eggs. They were horrible
things, and Ben couldn't get past them quickly
enough. He kicked his legs harder and pushed
for the surface.

They emerged in the same room where
Grandpa Max had popped up. Above them were

the metal walkways. This time, though, there wasn't one alien standing on guard, there were dozens! The creatures snarled and spat, their eyes fixed on the intruders.

'We are not stealthy,' Ben muttered.

Kevin cracked his knuckles. 'But we kick much butt.'

On cue, Ben punched the dial of the Omnitrix. In a flash of glowing green, he transformed into a spindly blue alien, wearing what looked like a tattered robe. The robe unfolded, revealing itself to be a pair of huge, moth-like wings.

'Big Chill!' hissed the alien hero, as Gwen and Kevin both leapt from the pool.

Kevin paused to absorb the strength of the iron walkway, turning his body into living metal. He kicked out wildly, catching one DNAlien in the stomach, and sending him spinning into another gang of the hideous creatures. The whole group toppled to the ground like skittles.

Big Chill swooped down. He flew
straight through five of the DNAliens, one at
a time, passing through them as if he was a
ghost. As he phased in and out of them, each
alien found itself frozen solid and completely
unable to move.

'I thought you guys liked it cold,' laughed
Big Chill.

Gwen was blasting her way through
another group of the creatures. Her power
blasts took care of four, five, six of the aliens,

slamming into them and forcing them to
their knees.

A seventh alien lunged at her, but she
was too fast. A bolt of pink energy crackled
from her fingertips and struck the creature
on the chest. As it fell, she realised there was
something different about this alien. Something
strangely familiar . . .

From nowhere, Kevin made a dive for the
DNAlien, his fists raised. Just before he could
deliver the knock-out blow, an energy shield
forced him back.

'Wait!' cried Gwen. 'Get back. Get away
from him!'

Freezing the last of the remaining aliens,
Big Chill glided down on to the walkway beside
Kevin. He gasped as the DNAlien lifted his head
to reveal a partially human face.

'It's Ken,' Gwen said. 'It's my brother.'

Green light swept across Big Chill,
changing him back into Ben. He studied the

DNAlien's face, barely able to believe what he was seeing.

'You're right,' he nodded. 'It is Ken.'

'That's Ken?' snorted Kevin, looking down at the twisted form of the half-human, half-alien. 'He's actually less cool than his car.'

'We've got to help him,' insisted Gwen.

'He was fighting us,' Ben reminded her. 'Whatever they did to him affected his mind.'

Ken touched the Xenocyte that was covering most of his face. A tear rolled down from his one human eye. 'What this did to m-me,' he began, before his voice grew deeper and his face darkened, 'is set me free!'

Snarling, Ken snatched up the fallen body of another DNAlien. He roared as he hurled the lifeless alien towards Ben. Dodging to the side, Ben raised his fists. He didn't want to fight Ken, but he would if he had to.

'Let's get him,' cried Kevin.

'No, don't hurt him,' pleaded Gwen. 'He's just sick.'

Ken shrieked with rage as his sister wrapped him in energy tendrils, holding him in place. 'It's that thing on him. It's making him do this.'

Kevin pushed forward and took hold of the wriggling Xenocyte. 'Then let's get it off him.' Gritting his teeth, he pulled the creature. A scream of pain burst from Ken's lips.

'Kevin, wait,' Ben yelped, pulling Kevin away. 'You're hurting him!'

As Ben drew close to Ken, the Omnitrix began to flash a worrying shade of red.

'Severe genetic damage detected,' chimed

a voice from inside the watch.

Cautiously, Ben lifted the device nearer his mouth. 'Hello?' he whispered. 'Uh, Omnitrix, is that you?'

'Genetic code splicing error,' continued the watch. 'Should we attempt to repair?'

Ben glanced at his half-alien cousin. 'Try to fix Ken? Yeah. Let's do it!'

Placing his hand on the writhing Xenocyte, Ben felt a buzz of energy spread out from inside the Omnitrix. It seemed to pass through him and into the alien parasite.

'What are you doing?' asked his worried cousin, Gwen.

Ben shrugged. 'I'm not entirely sure.'

Two of the Xenocyte's tentacles thrashed up and attached themselves to Ben's face. He screwed his eyes tightly closed as they slithered across his cheeks and probed at his nostrils.

When Ben opened his eyes he almost cried out in shock. He was no longer in the hatchery. Instead he was floating down a long tunnel. The walls glowed a familiar shade of green, and he realised at once where he was.

Whoa. I'm inside the Omnitrix, he thought. A giant image of Ken's head floated along the tunnel, the Xenocyte still wrapped around it. And so was the creepy-crawly.

Ben floated onwards until he was level with the bug-alien's bulging green eye. He dug his fingers into the creature's gooey flesh and pulled. It was horrible, but he had to save Ken. He was going to save Ken.

With a soft, gloopy **SCHLOP**, hundreds of smaller tentacles began to grow from the Xenocyte's skin. They twisted and curled up Ben's arms. They wrapped around his body, around his neck, around his head.

Ben tried to scream for help, but it was too late. The tentacles cocooned him completely, and he found himself suffocating in cold, black darkness.

CHAPTER FIVE

FACING THE HIGHBREED

Ben opened his eyes. He was standing in the hatchery, Gwen and Kevin by his side. Something cold and wet was in his hand, and he realised he was holding the limp body of the Xenocyte.

Ken was on his hands and knees on the floor, groaning. The alien was no longer attached to him. He was human once more.

Ben dropped the creature and examined the Omnitrix. 'I'm going to have to get a manual for this thing,' he muttered. He smiled at his cousin. 'It's OK, Ken. Everything's going to be just fine.'

'Nothing's fine,' Ken wheezed. 'I captured Grandpa. Handed him over to them. I-I couldn't stop. It was like I was watching someone else doing it.'

'They have Grandpa Max?' Ben quizzed.

'That's why they took me. They knew he'd come for me.'

Ben glanced around at the others. 'Let's go get him.'

Ken gritted his teeth and pulled himself up. His legs wobbled, but he refused to fall. 'I'm coming with you,' he announced.

'You want to help?' asked Kevin, impressed by Ken's determination. 'Cool.'

On the floor of the control room, Max raised his head. The door was sliding open, and he had no idea what might come through. His arms and legs were tied. There would be nothing he could do to defend himself.

His face folded into a smile of relief when

he saw who stepped through the door.

'Ben!'

'Grandpa Max,' Ben replied, rushing over to untie his grandfather's bonds.

'You're a sight for sore eyes,' Max told him. He stood up as the ropes fell away, just in time for Gwen to trap him in a hug.

'I'm so glad you're OK,' she whispered.

Max smiled. 'Me too, honey.' The old man turned and faced Gwen's brother. 'Kenny.'

'Grandpa. I didn't know what I was doing,' Ken sobbed. 'I . . . I . . .'

Max's strong arms slipped around the boy's shoulders, pulling him into a warm bear-hug. 'It's OK,' he said, softly.

Grandpa Max turned to his other grandson. 'I always knew you could do it, Ben,' he smiled. 'I'm so proud of you. All of you.' Max nodded over to Kevin, who was standing a little away from the others. 'You too, Kevin. I've been watching. You've come a long way. Might even earn that Plumber's badge you swiped.'

Suddenly, a crackly voice boomed out from the control room's speaker systems.

'Attention all personnel,' announced the voice of the HighBreed, 'initiate Project DNA now.'

With a series of clanks and whirrs, the entire hatchery building seemed to come to life. Ben and the others raced to a window, where they saw long floating vehicles vacuuming Xenocyte eggs up from the liquid-filled trenches. The egg-carriers then continued on to where hundreds of DNAliens were waiting to load the eggs on to trucks.

'What are they doing?' whispered Ben.

'They're shipping those things somewhere,' Grandpa told him. 'Putting together a DNAlien army.' Max spun to face his grandson. His expression was deadly serious. 'Stop them, Ben. These Xenocytes must be destroyed. Go.'

With a nod, Ben sprinted for the door, Kevin, Gwen and Ken following hot on his heels.

Just before he left the control room, however, Ben stopped and looked back at his grandfather. 'What are you going to do?'

Max smiled, but it was a thin, sad smile. 'What I have to.'

KRAKKA-WHOOSH!

The first of the trucks went up in a blinding fireball, sparked by Gwen's power blasts. All around the complex, DNAliens stopped their egg-loading and swarmed to launch an attack.

Ben activated the Omnitrix, and leapt into the air as the swirling green energy wrapped around him, transforming him into Jet Ray. The flying alien gained height, then sharply banked down over the remaining trucks, zapping them with his neuroshock lasers.

BOOM!
BOOM!
BOOM!

Fuel tanks ignited one by one, destroying most of the vehicles and the terrible cargo inside them.

Absorbing the metal of a crowbar Ken had picked up, Kevin set to work battling the DNAliens. He punched and kicked furiously, sending the creatures flailing in all directions.

Meanwhile, Ken was putting the crowbar to work. He dodged and darted around the DNAliens, stopping only to smash any Xenocyte eggs he found. He would make sure they couldn't do to anyone else what they had done to him.

Several more DNAliens closed in on Gwen. Their claws swiped at her and their teeth snapped hungrily together. Gwen floated above them, pink energy buzzing behind her eyes.

'You kidnapped my brother. Turned him into a monster. Captured my grandfather.' Gwen's fingertips lit up like fireworks. 'I have had it with you!'

A ripple of energy exploded from inside her. It hit the approaching aliens like a shockwave, knocking them out and destroying the last few remaining trucks.

Jet Ray landed on the ground beside Kevin. In the blink of an eye he was Ben again. He watched his cousin, impressed.

'Wow,' he said.

Kevin nodded. 'Yeah.'

On the building behind them, a window was lit up by a series of blinding white flashes. Ben turned and ran towards the front door. The trucks may have been stopped, but Grandpa Max was still in danger.

Ben and the others hurried through the control room. Machinery lay smashed and scattered everywhere. Grandpa had been busy.

They pushed on through the door at the back of the room, then skidded to a stop. In the centre of the cavern-like room they had entered was a mountain of eggs. There must have been thousands of them – millions, maybe. Above the mound, a weird, insect-like alien laid another egg on to the pile every few seconds.

'So, was I right?' whispered Kevin.

Ben nodded, grimly. 'Yeah. Worst road trip ever.'

A frantic struggle over to his left caught Ben's attention. He looked over to see Max battling with the HighBreed. His Grandpa was using all his strength and skill, but the alien was easily fending him off.

With a screech of triumph, the HighBreed reached out and snatched Max up with one hand. His long, black fingers tightened around Grandpa's helpless body.

'Stay back,' hissed the HighBreed, 'or this one breathes no more.'

'Give it up, we've beaten you,' Ben shouted. 'Your factory's toast, your trucks are smashed. It's over.'

'Fools!' cackled the alien. 'More trucks can be here in a matter of hours. And my DNAlien hordes . . .' He gestured for them to look out of the window. A sea of DNAliens stood outside the building, surrounding it completely.

'Are already here,' Ben croaked.

'It ends now,' the HighBreed told him. 'Nowhere left to run.'

A grim smile spread across Grandpa Max's face. 'I wasn't running, chief. I was looking for the egg-machine.'

Max twisted his arm and reached into his pocket. The Null Void Projector glowed red as he held it up for the alien to see.

'A Null Void Projector. You think you can imprison us all?' snorted the HighBreed.

'No,' Grandpa Max admitted. He snapped the red cover off the weapon. 'But without the focusing lens, this thing'll do a pretty good imitation of a hand grenade. I figure it'll take out half a mile.'

The HighBreed hesitated. 'You wouldn't dare. You'd be destroyed. And your offspring.'

'Gwen,' Max called, 'throw up an energy shield around you and the boys and hold on tight.' He gave her an encouraging smile. 'And be a good girl.'

'Grandpa Max, no,' begged Ben, realising what was about to happen. 'Please!'

'Sorry, Ben. It's the only way to make sure they can't do to the rest of the world what they did to Ken. You'll have to take it from here. I know you can do it. I believe in you. All of you.'

Ben tried to run forwards, but Kevin caught him by his shirt. A shimmering energy shield flew up around them, just as Max's finger pressed down on the trigger. The explosion tore through the complex; a burst of pure white energy that vapourised everything in its path.

When the smoke cleared, the energy bubble was the only thing left standing for miles around. The hatchery, the HighBreed, even the army of DNAliens were all gone.

And so was Grandpa Max.

'Whoa,' Kevin croaked. 'That was pretty hardcore.'

The energy shield fizzled out, as tears began to roll down Gwen's cheeks. 'He . . . he saved the whole world,' she sobbed.

'Yeah, he did. For now,' said Ben, his

voice shaking. 'But those things aren't going to give up. It's up to someone to protect this planet.' Ben looked up at the dark night sky. It had stopped raining, but he knew the storm would not be far away. 'And like it or not, I think it's up to us!'

Don't Miss This!

The official Ben 10 magazine:
free gifts, posters, comic,
puzzles and more... every issue

Available from all good newsagents
and supermarkets